Lindsay Lee Johnson

HURRICANE HENRIETTA

pictures by Wally Neibart

Dial Books for Young Readers  New York

Published by Dial Books for Young Readers
A member of Penguin Putnam Inc.
375 Hudson Street
New York, New York 10014

Designed by Pamela Darcy
Printed in Hong Kong
First Edition
1 3 5 7 9 10 8 6 4 2

Library of Congress Cataloging in Publication Data
Johnson, Lindsay Lee.
Hurricane Henrietta/by Lindsay Lee Johnson; pictures by Wally Neibart.
p.   cm.
Summary: Henrietta's incredibly long hair causes her nothing but trouble until
Francine the hairdresser saves the day.
ISBN 0-8037-1976-0 (tr.)—ISBN 0-8037-1977-9 (lib. bdg.)
(1. Hair—Fiction. 2. Humorous stories.) I. Neibart, Wally, ill. II. Title.
PZ7.J632526Hu 1998 (E)—dc21 96-44436 CIP AC

The artwork for this book was prepared using pencil and watercolor.

For Mom, who did daily battle with
my own tangled tresses,
and for Jessie and Leisha
—L.L.J.

To my grandson, Samuel August Smith
—W.N.

Everyone in the town of Bald Eagle Falls knew Henrietta Harrison. Not only was she the bubble-blowing, hopscotching, rope-jumping champion of Adventure Scout Troop 417, Henrietta was famous for something she'd never done.

"I've never had my hair cut in my whole life," Henrietta boasted. "Not one hair."

At school Henrietta always had something unusual for show-and-tell. Every time she reached into her hair, she pulled out a surprise.

"More, more!" the students shouted. "Show us something else!"

During recess the kindergartners begged to play in Henrietta's hair. It was more fun than the jungle gym.

The best part of the day was walking home. When
Henrietta swept down the street, her hair billowed along
behind her. It made her shadow look very important.
Henrietta smiled and waved, like a queen riding by.

When Henrietta's hair grew past her knees, her picture
appeared in the papers. Everyone agreed it was remarkable.
Henrietta loved the attention.

As soon as Henrietta's hair reached her ankles, she
started making plans. "I'll have my own TV show," she said.
"Then there'll be Henrietta dolls."

And Henrietta's hair kept right on growing.

But as Henrietta's hair grew more famous, it also began to
cause trouble.

Because of Henrietta, everyone in her neighborhood started wearing crash helmets and life jackets. Even the dogs.

"Make way for Hurricane Henrietta!" people shouted, hanging on to lampposts.

There were places Henrietta couldn't go. "Don't even think about it!" said the ticket seller at the amusement park.

There were things Henrietta couldn't do. "We don't have your size, dear," said the swimming pool attendant, looking for a cap to fit Henrietta.

But the worst blow came the day Henrietta's hair got to be too much even for the Adventure Scouts. The troops were unprepared when Henrietta breezed in.

"Typhoon!" cried the scouts. "Alert the coast guard!"

The troop leader, Ms. Riggs, reached for her whistle, but already it had been swallowed by Henrietta's hungry hair.

"You'll need a compass and a rescue dog to find your way out of your tent at Safari Camp next week," said Ms. Riggs, pulling her butterfly net from behind Henrietta's ear. "You'd better go see Francine the hairdresser."

"Not scissors-happy Francine!" cried Henrietta. "There's got to be another way!"

"Something must be done about that hair," Ms. Riggs said. "Before camp."

"I'll take care of it," Henrietta promised. But how, she wondered?

At home Henrietta's mother and little brother Arnold were waiting on the front steps.

"My guinea pig is gone!" cried Arnold. "And it's all your fault!"

"Not again," groaned Henrietta.

Henrietta's mother plucked fourteen yo-yos, three kites, and a banjo from Henrietta's hair before she found Arnold's squealing guinea pig. "It's time to do something about that hair," she said.

Henrietta brushed her hair a thousand times, smoothing it out flat, but when she got caught in the rain, her curls fanned out like a flock of blackbirds.

"Dive-bombers!" people shouted. "Take cover!"

Tired and discouraged, Henrietta went home to bed. Her hair curled around her like a nest.

In the morning Henrietta's dark waves were tumbling and churning like a thunderstorm about to break.

"Time for a shampoo," said Henrietta's mother.

"Ugh!" said Henrietta.

But Henrietta's hair had outgrown the bathtub.

Putting it in the washing machine was too messy.

"No way!" said Henrietta.

Sending Henrietta to the dry cleaners took too long.

Finally Henrietta had to ride through the car wash. With the top down.

"Wow!" said Arnold. "You look like a movie star!"

Henrietta beamed. Then Arnold told her the movie he had in mind was *Return of the Human Hair-Ball*.

"Hmmmph!" snorted Henrietta. She wrapped her head in a towering turban. "This ought to do the trick," she said.

But when Henrietta's mother sent her out to do the marketing, a brisk wind caught one end of the turban. It spun Henrietta like a tornado. Her hair broke loose again, whipping the outdoor market into a giant tossed salad.

"It's raining rutabagas!" people screamed.

"Artichoke attack!"

"Eggplant alert!"

Back at home
Henrietta's mother
said, "You won't be
able to take care of
that hair out in the
woods. You'll come
home with birds
and squirrels
nesting around
your ears."

Arnold snickered.
Henrietta wailed. "But I've saved all
my Adventure Scout cookie money for Safari Camp!"

"No Safari Camp," said Henrietta's mother, "until you tame
that mane!"

Henrietta was running out of ideas. She finally decided
she had to ask the expert.

Henrietta laced up her skates and sped off to see
Francine the hairdresser at the Bald Eagle Hair
Salon.

Armed with brushes and combs, ribbons, hairpins, and
barrettes, Francine tackled Henrietta's wayward locks.

After hours of pigtails, ponytails, braids, twists, and buns,
Francine's arms were aching. "It's no use," she said at last.
She reached for the shears, but Henrietta panicked and
bolted from the chair.

"I'm out of here!" she cried.

Henrietta nearly escaped, but her hair got caught in the revolving door, just as Harry the wig salesman was coming into the salon to show his new collection.

"My wigs!" cried Harry. "You've squashed them!"

"My hair!" cried Henrietta. "I'm trapped!"

Brandishing her scissors, Francine caught up with Henrietta.

"Hold still," she said. "I'll just take a little off the top."

"Not so fast!" cried Harry. "If you cut her hair, you'll shred my wigs!"

Henrietta sniffed at the fake locks that were entwined with her own. "What are these wigs made of?" she asked. "They're not real hair."

"Recycled mops and scouring pads," said Harry proudly.

Henrietta thought hard for a moment. "I have an idea," she said. "Maybe we can make a deal. I'm ready now, Francine," she said bravely.

Harry covered his eyes. "What will happen to my wigs?" he moaned. "I can't watch!"

Francine began to snip.
It took hours.

A crowd gathered outside the Bald Eagle Hair Salon.
When Francine finally put down the shears, everyone
stepped up to take a look.

"Splendid!" said Henrietta's mother.
"Becoming!" said Francine.

"Snazzy!" said the Adventure Scouts.
"Nifty!" admitted Arnold.

Nervously Henrietta peeked into a mirror.

"It's still me!" she declared.

Francine called in the street sweepers to clear away the mountains of hair on the floor.

"Hold on there!" Henrietta shouted. "That's my hair, and I'm giving it all to Harry."

Harry looked horrified for a moment. Then he grinned.

Using Henrietta's trimmings, Harry started a new business: *Henrietta's 100% Recycled Real Human Hair Wonder Wigs.* Everybody wanted one. Including Harry.

At Safari Camp, Henrietta hiked and swam and rode horseback, just like the other scouts.

Sometimes Henrietta missed all the excitement her long locks had caused. Secretly she enjoyed the nervous looks people gave her when she skipped an appointment for another haircut.

Luckily—Francine made housecalls.